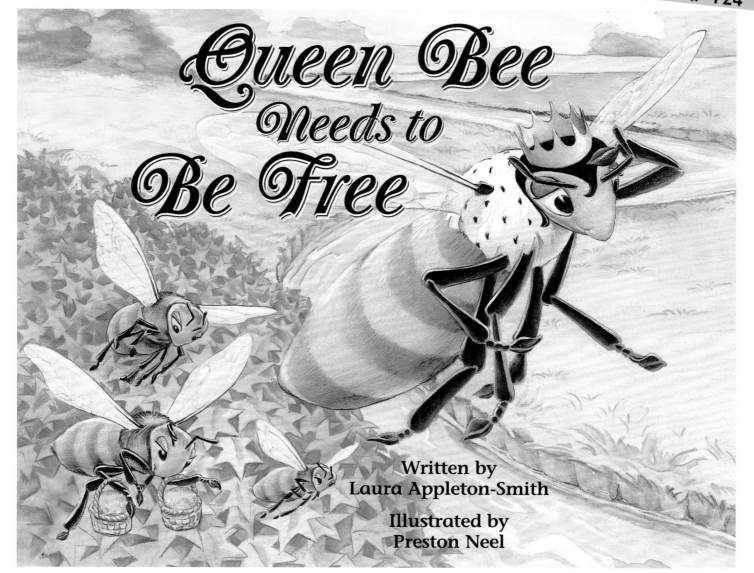

Queen Bee Needs to Be Free

Written by
Laura Appleton-Smith

Illustrated by
Preston Neel

Laura Appleton-Smith was born and raised in Vermont and holds a degree in English from Middlebury College. Laura is a primary school teacher who has combined her talents in creative writing and her experience in early childhood education to create *Books to Remember*. Laura lives in New Hampshire with her husband, Terry.

Preston Neel was born in Macon, Georgia. Greatly inspired by Dr. Seuss, he decided to become an artist at the age of four. Preston's advanced art studies took place at the Academy of Art College San Francisco. Now Preston pursues his career in art with the hope of being an inspiration himself, particularly to children who want to explore their endless bounds.

A Book to Remember™
Published by Flyleaf Publishing

For orders or information, contact us at **(800) 449-7006**.
Please visit our website at **www.flyleafpublishing.com**

Eighth Edition 2/20
Library of Congress Catalog Card Number: 2005935764
ISBN-13: 978-1-929262-43-4
Printed and bound in the USA
243081021A24

For my Mom, thank you, as always, for your loving support.

LAS

For my Queen, I will drone on forever.

PN

Chapter One

Once upon a time there was a wild honeybee nest hidden in the trunk of an old Sweet Gum tree.

2

In the nest lived the Queen Bee.

The Queen's needs were tended to
by the rest of the bees in the colony.

The attendant bees would feed the Queen
a diet of honey and royal jelly.

4

The attendants would fan the Queen when she got hot and they would tidy up after her if there was a mess or not. Their duty was to be kind.

Chapter Two

Because of the Queen's diet, she was bigger than the rest of the bees in the colony.

She was also the only bee that was able to lay eggs.

The Queen dropped hundreds of eggs into wax combs.

The attendants would tend to the eggs
until they developed into adult bees.

It would seem that in a bee colony
a queen would be the best bee to be—
being swept up after and fed and fanned and all...

But the difficult fact of being a queen is that
queen bees almost never get to exit their nests.
The queen exits the nest once to breed so she can lay eggs.
She only exits once more if there is a swarm.

What is a swarm, you ask?
A swarm happens when a bee's nest is overfilled.
It is a queen's instinct to split the colony
so the nest is not so full of bees.

The queen exits the nest with a lot of attendants
to find a spot to construct a new colony.

The rest of the bees keep on living in the old nest.
They grant the title of "Queen" to a new queen bee.

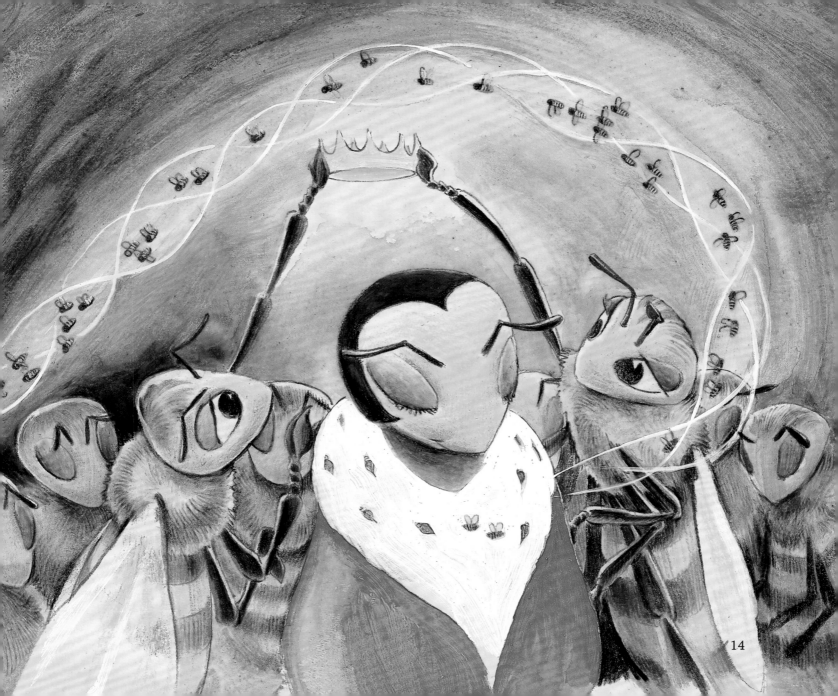

Chapter Three

In the colony in the Sweet Gum tree,
the attendant bees could see that their Queen
seemed restless. "I feel the need to be free,"
said the Queen Bee.

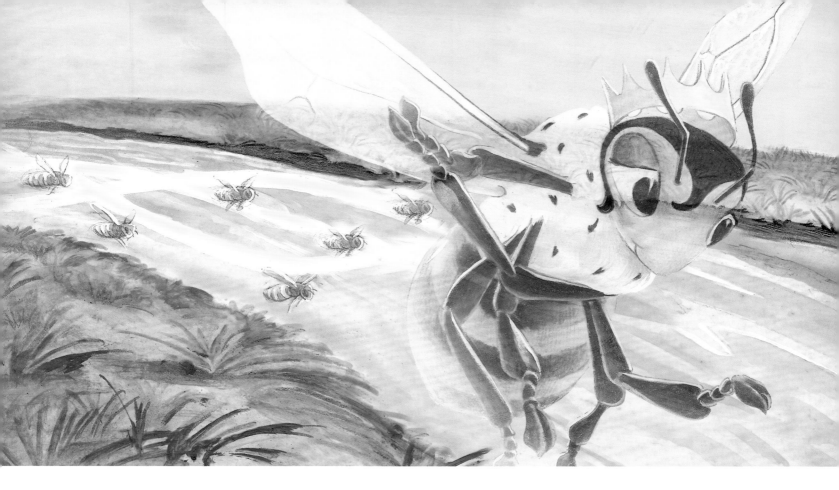

"I long to see the land beyond the Sweet Gum tree.
I long to see the sunlight and the grass so gold and green,"
buzzed the Queen.

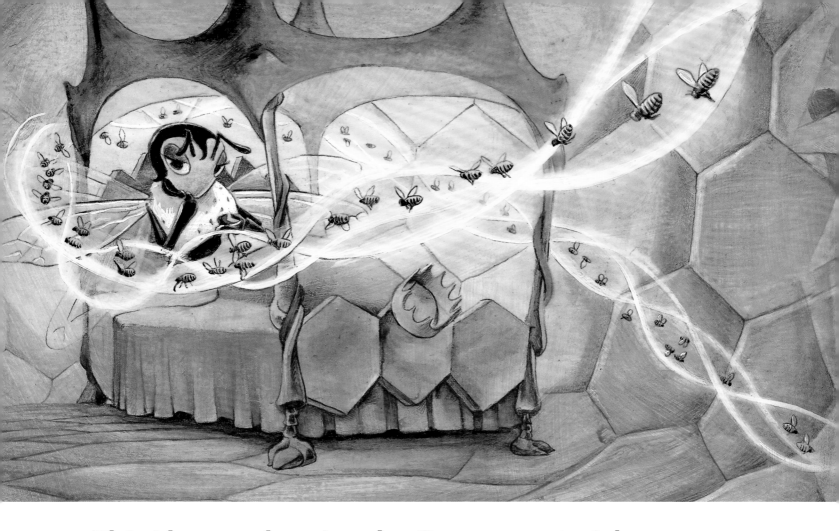

This idea was keeping the Queen up at night.
She did not feel right. She sat up in bed humming
and buzzing and tapping her feet.

The truth was that the Queen Bee had been visited by her instinct. Her instinct told her that she must swarm.

The Queen Bee emitted a pheromone.
This pheromone told the rest of the bees
that she planned to swarm.

The opening of the nest was filled with bees.
Hundreds of bees wiggled and spun and buzzed
and hummed. The swarm had begun.

Chapter Four

As the queen set off on her flight, she buzzed with glee,
"See the bright sunlight on the grass so gold and green?
Can you smell the fragrant milkweed?
This is super! We are finally free!"

The swarm rested high up in a tree.

The attendants clustered around
the Queen to protect her.

The scout bees went off to find a spot
to construct a new nest.

The swarm rested in the tree for almost three days.

On the last day the bees spotted a human.
The man was a beekeeper. He put a box under the tree.

The beekeeper jiggled the tree.
Lots of attendant bees and
the Queen fell into the box.

The attendant bees did not mind the beekeeper's box.
It was a good spot to construct a nest.

When the scout bees got back they agreed.
Every bee felt that the box was truly the right spot
for the new colony.

By nightfall, most of the bees from the swarm were in the box.

The beekeeper was glad to see that the wild bees had picked his box for their new nest.

The Queen no longer felt restless.

Now her instinct told her to lay eggs in the nest so there would be lots of new bees to make honey for the colony and for the beekeeper and his family.

Glossary

Attendants
Attendant bees are also called worker bees.
They take care of the queen and the colony.

Beekeeper
A beekeeper is a person who
raises bees.

Colony
A bee colony is a big group of bees
living in one place with one queen.

Combs
Combs are six-sided cells built by bees out of wax.
Combs are where bees store their food and raise their young.

Honey
A sweet, thick fluid made by bees from plant nectar.

Honeybee
A honeybee is a bee that makes honey.

Instinct
A strong feeling that animals are born with that tells them to act in a certain way
without even thinking about it.

Pheromones
Instead of communicating with words, like people do, bees communicate with pheromones.
Pheromones are messages that are picked up by a bee's sense of smell.

Queen Bee

The queen bee is the mother of all the bees in the colony. She is bigger than all of the other bees.

Royal Jelly

The only food fed to a developing queen bee. Royal jelly is also fed to the rest of the young bees in the colony, but unlike the queen, it is not the only food they eat while developing.

Scout Bees

Bees that hunt for a spot to construct a new nest.

Swarm

A group of bees, with a queen bee, moving to set up a new colony. A swarm is the way that a new bee colony is started.

Wax

Wax is a solid, yellowish substance that bees make their honeycombs out of.

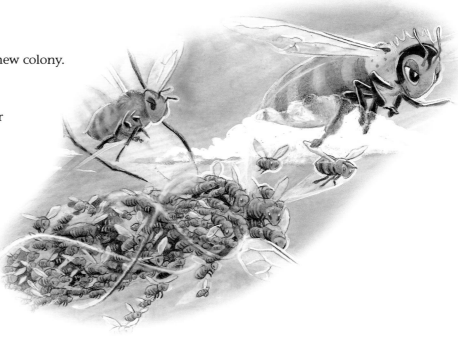

Prerequisite Skills

Single consonants and short vowels
Final double consonants **ff**, **gg**, **ll**, **nn**, **ss**, **tt**, **zz**
Consonant /k/ **ck**
/ng/ **n[k]**
Consonant digraphs /ng/ **ng**, /th/ **th**, /hw/ **wh**
Schwa /ə/ **a**, **e**, **i**, **o**, **u**
Long /ē/ **ee**, **y**
r-Controlled /ûr/ **er**
/ô/ **al**, **all**
/ul/ **le**
/d/ or /t/ **–ed**

Target Letter-Sound Correspondence
Long /ā/ sound spelled **a**

a
able
fragrant

Target Letter-Sound Correspondence
Long /ī/ sound spelled **igh**

bright	nightfall
flight	right
high	sunlight
night	

Target Letter-Sound Correspondence
Long /ē/ sound spelled **e**

be	emitted
begun	he
being	idea
beyond	we
developed	

Target Letter-Sound Correspondences
Patterns **ild**, **ind**

find	mind
kind	wild

Target Letter-Sound Correspondence
Long /ī/ sound spelled **i**

diet	tidy
finally	title
idea	

Target Letter-Sound Correspondence

Long /ō/ sound spelled **o**

opening	protect
overfilled	so

Target Letter-Sound Correspondences

Patterns **old, ost**

gold	old
most	told

Target Letter-Sound Correspondences

Long /ū/ and long /o͞o/ sounds spelled **u**

duty	truly
human	truth
super	

Story Puzzle Words

chapter	pheromone
combs	royal
honey	scout
honeybee	swarm
lay	

High-Frequency Puzzle Words

are	now
around	of
because	once
been	one
by	only
could	or
day	put
days	said
every	she
for	their
four	there
from	they
full	time
good	to
into	two
lived	was
living	were
make	what
more	would
new	you

Decodable Words

1	bees	feed	hundreds	nest	spun
2	best	feel	I	nests	sweet
3	bigger	feet	if	never	swept
4	box	fell	in	no	tapping
adult	breed	felt	instinct	not	tend
after	but	filled	is	off	tended
agreed	buzzed	free	it	on	than
all	buzzing	get	jelly	picked	that
almost	can	glad	jiggled	planned	the
also	clustered	glee	keep	Queen	this
an	colony	got	keeping	Queen's	three
and	construct	grant	land	rest	tree
as	did	grass	last	rested	trunk
ask	difficult	green	long	restless	under
at	dropped	gum	longer	sat	until
attendant	eggs	had	lot	see	up
attendants	exit	happens	lots	seem	upon
back	exits	her	man	seemed	visited
bed	fact	hidden	mess	set	wax
bee	family	his	milkweed	smell	went
bee's	fan	hot	must	split	when
beekeeper	fanned	hummed	need	spot	wiggled
beekeeper's	fed	humming	needs	spotted	with